Pippa's NIGHT Parade

BY
Lisa Robinson

ILLUSTRATED BY
Lucy Fleming

two lions

For Zoe and Naomi,
whose nighttime antics
inspired this story
—L.R.

For little Lola
—L.F.

Published by Two Lions, New York | www.apub.com
Amazon, the Amazon logo, and Two Lions are trademarks of Amazon.com,
Inc., or its affiliates.

ISBN-13: 9781542093002 (hardcover) | ISBN-10: 1542093007 (hardcover)
The illustrations are rendered in digital media.
Book design by Abby Dening
Printed in China | First Edition | 10 9 8 7 6 5 4 3 2 1

Pippa has a wonderfully wild imagination, but sometimes it runs a little TOO wild. That's when Pippa gets worried.

To prepare for each day,
Pippa puts on her armor.

MIGHTY masks.

BOLD boots.

SPUNKY scarves.

READY OR NOT, HERE SHE COMES!

But at night, Pippa falls
asleep worrying about

VILLAINS
AND
MONSTERS
AND
BEASTS.

One night, just as she closes her eyes—

SCRITCH, SCRATCH, SCREEEEEEECH!

It's a dragon! Clawing out of a storybook.

Pippa tries extra night-lights.

Pippa ties triple knots.

Pippa designs
a disguise.

Pippa sprints to her parents' room.
Daddy brings her back to bed.

Again

and again

and again.

Everyone is terribly tired . . .
except the **VILLAINS**,
who never tire of being terrible.

DANGER

Pippa needs a plan.
Maybe if she summons them all at once,
she can get rid of them once and for all.

The next day, Pippa slips an invitation into every book on the shelf.

WHAT: Scary Night parade
WHEN: TONIGHT
WHERE: Pippa's Room

SHARPEN YOUR CLAWS!
PREPARE YOUR FUR and PAWS!
COME SCARE THE PANTS OFF Pippa!

Pippa plots and plans.

That night,
the bookshelf
rumbles.

WITCHES

AND
ZOMBIES

AND
GHOSTS

tumble out
of the books.

Pippa tries everything:

lasso for the
Loch Ness Monster,

eye patch for the Cyclops,

sun hat for the serpent.

VICTORY!

But the BEASTS and BRUTES and BADDIES
keep on coming.

DEFEAT!

PIPPA'S
DESIGN
STUDIO

Pippa retreats.
She needs a new plan.

To prepare for battle, Pippa pulls out everything she's got:

sashes and sequins and bows,

belts and berets and shawls.

She rips and tears, stitches and sews,
glues and snaps. . . .

READY OR NOT,

HERE SHE COMES!

The troll grumbles.
The witch grimaces.
The lion growls.

. . . But then the creatures
survey the carnival of costumes,
and they begin to pose and primp and preen.

"Line up and strut your stuff!" says Pippa.
"Chin out. Shoulders back. Hips forward."

Now every night, the villains spring off the shelves
and sashay through a spectacular show.

When they are worn out by
the pompous parading around,
they curl up to catch some rest . . .

including Pippa,
who sleeps beautifully ever after.